Sunset of the Sabretooth

Jack read the writing below the picture of the cave. It said:

> *The great cave bears of the Ice Age were over two metres tall. These bears were larger and fiercer than today's grizzlies. Their caves were filled with the bones of their ancestors.*

"Annie!" whispered Jack. "Get back here now!"

They were in the cave of a great cave bear!

Look out for these other books in the
Magic Tree House series:

Dinosaurs Before Dark
The Knight at Dawn
Mummies in the Morning
Pirates Past Noon
Night of the Ninjas
Afternoon on the Amazon

Coming soon:
Midnight on the Moon

Join the Magic Tree House Club.
See back of book for details.

Sunset of the Sabretooth

Mary Pope Osborne

Illustrated by Sal Murdocca

SCHOLASTIC

To all the kids who've helped me

Scholastic Children's Books,
Commonwealth House, 1–19 New Oxford Street,
London WC1A 1NU, UK
a division of Scholastic Ltd
London ~ New York ~ Toronto ~ Sydney ~ Auckland
Mexico City ~ New Delhi ~ Hong Kong

Published by arrangement with Random House Children's Books,
a division of Random House Inc.
First published in the UK by Scholastic Ltd, 2000

Text copyright © Mary Pope Osborne, 1995
Illustrations copyright © Sal Murdocca, 1995

ISBN 0 439 99616 3

Printed by The Bath Press, Bath

2 4 6 8 10 9 7 5 3 1

Contents

Prologue

One summer day in Frog Creek, Pennsylvania, a mysterious tree house appeared in the woods.

Eight-year-old Jack and his seven-year-old sister, Annie, climbed into the tree house. They found that it was filled with books.

Jack and Annie soon discovered that the tree house was magic. It could take them to the places in the books. All they had to do was point to a picture and wish to go there.

Jack and Annie visited dinosaurs, knights, an Egyptian queen, pirates, ninjas and the Amazon rain forest.

Along the way, they discovered that the tree house belonged to Morgan le Fay. Morgan was a magical librarian. She travelled through time and space, gathering books for King Arthur's library.

On their fifth adventure, *Night of the Ninjas*, Jack and Annie found a little mouse in the tree house. Annie named their new friend "Peanut".

Jack and Annie also found a note from Morgan. The note told them that she was under a spell. To free her, Jack and Annie must find four special things.

They found the first thing in old Japan, and the second in the Amazon rain forest.

Now Jack and Annie and Peanut are about to set out in search of the third thing . . . in *Sunset of the Sabretooth.*

1

The "M" Things

"Let's go to the tree house," said Annie.

She and Jack were passing the Frog Creek woods on their way home from their swimming class at the sports centre.

"No. I want to go home and change out of my swimming-trunks," said Jack.

"Oh, that'll take too long," said Annie. "Don't you want to save Morgan as soon as possible?"

"Of course," said Jack.

"Then come on! Before the sun sets!" said Annie.

She darted into the woods.

Jack sighed. He gave up on the idea of changing out of his swimming trunks.

He pushed his glasses into place. He followed Annie into the Frog Creek woods.

The warm air smelled fresh and green.

He moved through patches of sunlight and shadow. Soon he came to a small clearing.

He looked up. There it was. The magic tree house in the tallest tree in the woods.

"Hurry!" called Annie. She was climbing the rope-ladder up to the tree house.

Jack grabbed the ladder. He climbed up after her.

Finally they reached the tree house.

Squeak. A mouse sat on the window-sill.

"Hi, Peanut!" cried Annie.

Jack patted the tiny head.

"Sorry we didn't come sooner," Annie said. "But we had to go to our swimming lesson."

Squeak.

"What happened while we were gone?" asked Annie, looking around the tree house.

Jack stared at the large M carved into the wooden floor.

On the M were a moonstone and a mango, the special things they'd found on their last two journeys.

"Hey, guess what?" said Jack. "*Moonstone* and *mango* start with the letter M. Just like *Morgan*."

"You're right," said Annie.

"I bet all four things start with an M," said Jack.

"Right," said Annie. "I wonder where we'll find the next one."

She and Jack stared at the stacks of books in the tree house. Books on the Amazon rain forest, ninjas, pirates, mummies, knights and dinosaurs.

All of them were closed. Only one book lay open in the corner.

"We're just about to find out," said Jack.

They walked over to the open book.

They looked at the page the book was opened to. It showed a picture of rocks and snow.

"Wow," said Annie, running her finger over the picture. "I love snow. I wish we could go there right now."

"Wait," said Jack. "We're not prepared." Then he had another thought. "And we're wearing our swimming-costumes! Stop!"

"Oops," said Annie.

Too late. The wind started to blow.

The leaves started to shake.

The tree house started to spin.
It spun faster and faster!
Then everything was silent.
It was as silent as the falling snow.

2

Bones

Jack, Annie and Peanut looked outside.

Snow was falling from a grey sky.

The tree house was in the tallest tree in a grove of tall bare trees.

The grove was on a wide white plain. Beyond the plain were high rocky cliffs.

"I'm c-cold," said Annie. Her teeth chattered. She wrapped her towel tightly around her.

Sq-squeak. Peanut sounded cold, too.

"Poor mouse," said Annie. "I'll put you into Jack's bag. You'll be warmer there."

Annie slipped Peanut into the pocket of the rucksack.

"We have to go home," said Jack. "We need warmer clothes."

"We can't go home," said Annie. "We can't find the Pennsylvania book. Not until our mission is complete. Remember? That's the way the magic works."

"Oh . . . right," said Jack. He looked around. There was no sign of the Pennsylvania book that always took them home.

Annie peered out of the window again. "Where are we, anyway?" she asked.

"I'll find out," said Jack. He picked up the open book and read the title on the cover. "*Life in the Ice Age*".

"*Ice Age?*" said Annie. "No wonder we're cold."

"We better find the third M thing soon," said Jack. "Before we freeze to death."

"Look," whispered Annie, "people." She pointed out of the window.

Jack saw them, too: four figures on a cliff. Two big figures and two little ones – all holding long spears.

"Who are they?" said Annie.

"I'll look in the book," said Jack.

He found a picture of some people. He read the caption to Annie:

Early modern humans were called Cro-Magnons. During the late Ice Age in Europe, they sometimes lived in caves beneath cliffs.

"Why are they carrying spears?" said Annie.

Jack turned the page. He found another picture of the Cro-Magnons. He read aloud:

> The Cro-Magnon family often hunted together. They covered deep pits with branches. Then they drove reindeer and mammoths into the traps.

"Oh, trapping the animals – that's sad," said Annie.

"No, it's not," said Jack. "They couldn't live without hunting. They didn't have supermarkets, you know."

They watched the family disappear over the other side of the cliff.

"Come on, I'm freezing," said Jack. "Let's hurry and find the M thing while the Cro-Magnons are hunting."

"But I want to meet them," said Annie.

"Forget it," said Jack. "They don't have books that tell them about *us*. They'll think we're some enemy and hurl their spears."

"Yikes," said Annie.

Jack put his book away.

Squeak. Peanut peeked out of the rucksack.

"Stay in there," said Annie.

Jack pulled on his pack and climbed down the rope-ladder.

Annie followed.

They huddled together on the icy ground.

The wind was biting. Jack put his towel over his head. Snow blew against his glasses.

"Hey, Jack," said Annie. "Look at me."

Annie had put on her swimming goggles. "Now I can see," she said.

"Good thinking," said Jack. "Now

cover your head with your towel. Most of your body heat is lost through your head."

Annie wrapped her towel around her head.

"We should find a cave or somewhere warmer," said Jack.

"I bet there are caves in those cliffs," said Annie.

She and Jack trudged across the white plain. The snow wasn't deep yet. But the wind was blowing hard.

"I told you!" Annie pointed to an opening in the rocks – a *cave*.

They ran to it.

"Watch out," said Jack. They stepped carefully into the shadowy cave.

It was only slightly warmer inside. But at least the wind wasn't blowing.

In the grey light, they stamped the snow off their trainers.

Annie took off her goggles.

"It smells in here," said Jack.

"Yeah, like a wet dog," said Annie.

"Let me see what I can find out," said Jack.

He pulled out the Ice Age book.

"I'll look around," said Annie. "Maybe the M thing is here. Then we can go home and get warm."

Jack stood by the entrance so he could read the book.

"This cave is filled with sticks," Annie said.

"What?" said Jack. He didn't look up from the book.

"No, wait. I think they're *bones*," said Annie.

"Bones?" echoed Jack.

"Yeah. Lots of them back here. All over the floor."

Jack turned the pages of his book. He found a picture of a cave filled with bones.

"I hear something," said Annie.

Jack read the writing below the picture of the cave. It said:

The great cave bears of the Ice Age were over two metres tall. These bears were larger and fiercer than today's grizzlies. Their caves were filled with the bones of their ancestors.

"Annie!" whispered Jack. "Get back here now!"

They were in the cave of a great cave bear!

3

Brrr!

"Annie!" whispered Jack again.

No answer.

He put his book quietly into his bag. He stepped deeper into the cave.

"Annie!" he said a little louder.

Jack stepped on the bones.

The wet dog smell grew stronger.

He kept going, deeper into the smelly blackness.

He ran into something. He gasped.

"Jack?" said Annie. "Is that you?"

"Didn't you hear me calling?" Jack whispered. "We have to get out of here!"

"Wait," she said. "Someone's sleeping back there. Hear him snoring?"

Jack heard a low, deep moaning. It was loud, then soft. Loud, then soft.

"That's not a person," he said. "It's a great cave bear!"

A booming snore shattered the air.

"Yikes!" said Annie.

"Go! Go!" said Jack.

He and Annie ran through the cave, over the bones and out into the falling snow.

They kept on going. They ran between fallen rocks and under jagged cliffs.

Finally they stopped and turned around.

All they could see was snow and rocks and their own footprints.

No bear.

26

"Phew," said Annie. "That was lucky."

"Yeah," said Jack. "He probably never even woke up. We just got in a panic."

Annie huddled close to Jack. "Brrr! I'm f-freezing," she said.

"Me too," he said.

He took off his glasses to wipe off the snow. The cold wind blew against his bare legs.

"Wow," Annie said. "Look." She pointed to something behind Jack.

"What?" Jack put his glasses back on and turned around.

Under a cliff was a wide ledge. Under the ledge was another cave.

Only *this* cave seemed to have a golden glow.

This one looked cosy and safe and warm.

4

Cave Kids

Jack and Annie crept to the cave and peeked inside.

A small flame danced from a bed of glowing coals.

Near the fire were knives, axes and hollowed-out stones.

Animal skins were neatly stacked against the wall.

"People must live here," said Annie.

"Maybe it's the home of the

Cro-Magnons we saw," said Jack, looking around.

"Let's go inside and get warm," said Annie.

Jack and Annie moved quickly to the fire and warmed their hands.

Their shadows danced on the stone walls.

Jack pulled out his Ice Age book. He found a picture of a cave. He read:

Cro-Magnons made many things from animals, plants and stone. They made flute-like musical instruments from mammoth bones. They made ropes by braiding plant fibres. They made axes and knives from stone.

Jack pulled out his notebook and pencil. He started a list:

Cro-Magnons made:
bone flutes
plant ropes
stone axes and knives

"Ta-da!" said Annie.

Jack looked up. Annie was wearing a coat.

It had a hood and long sleeves. It went all the way down to her trainers.

"Where did you get that?" said Jack.

"From that pile of furry skins," said Annie, pointing. "These must be their clothes. Maybe they're being mended."

She picked up another coat and handed it to Jack.

"Try one. It's really warm," she said.

Jack put his rucksack and towel down on the hard dirt floor. He slipped on the coat.

It did feel very warm – and soft.

"We look like cave kids," said Annie.

Squeak. Peanut peeked out of Jack's bag lying on the floor.

"You stay in there," said Annie. "There's no teeny coat for you."

Peanut vanished back into the bag.

"I wonder how they made these coats," said Jack.

He turned the pages in the book until he found a picture of Cro-Magnon women sewing. He read:

Cro-Magnons scraped reindeer skins with flint rocks to make them soft. They used bone needles to sew the skins together for clothing.

Jack added to his list:

reindeer-skin clothes

"I hope the cave people won't mind if we borrow their coats," said Jack.

"Maybe we should give them our towels," said Annie. "To thank them."

"Good idea."

"And my goggles, too," said Annie.

They left their gifts on top of the rest of the animal skins.

"Let's explore the cave before they come home," said Jack.

"It's too dark in the back," said Annie. "We won't be able to see anything."

"I'll find out how Cro-Magnons saw in the dark," said Jack.

He opened the Ice Age book. He found a picture of cave people holding odd-looking lamps. He read aloud to Annie:

Cro-Magnons made stone lamps. They hollowed out a rock, filled it with animal fat, then burned a wick made from moss.

"There!" said Annie. She pointed to two

stones near the fire. In the hollow of each was gooey white stuff and a pile of moss.

"We have to be careful," said Jack.

He picked up one stone. It was smaller than a soup bowl, but much heavier.

Jack held the stone close to the fire and lit the piece of moss.

He lit another lamp and gave it to Annie.

"Carry it with two hands," he said.

"I know," she said.

Jack tucked the book under his arm. He and Annie carried their stone lamps to the back of the cave.

"Hey, I wonder where this goes," said Annie. She held her lamp up to an opening in the wall.

"I'll check in the book," said Jack.

He put down his lamp and flipped through the Ice Age book.

"I think it's a tunnel," she said. "Be right back."

"Wait a second," said Jack.

Too late – she had squeezed into the opening and was gone.

"Oh great," said Jack, sighing.

He closed his book and peeked into the opening.

"Come back here!" he said.

"No! You come *here!*" said Annie. Her voice sounded far away. "You won't believe this!"

Jack picked up his lamp and book. He ducked into a small tunnel.

"Wow!" came Annie's voice.

Jack could see her lamp flickering at the other end.

Crouching down, he hurried towards her. At the end of the tunnel was a huge cavern with a high ceiling.

Annie held her lamp close to the wall.

"Look," she said. Her voice echoed.

Animals were painted on the wall in strokes of red and black and yellow.

There were cave bears and lions, elk and reindeer, bison and woolly rhinos and mammoths.

In the flickering light, the prehistoric beasts looked alive.

5

Snow Tracks

"Wow, what is this place?" said Jack.

"Maybe it's an art gallery," said Annie.

"I don't think so," said Jack. "It's too hard to get to."

He read about the cave paintings:

> These Ice Age beasts were painted
> 25,000 years ago. Cro-Magnons
> painted pictures of animals they
> hunted. They may have believed the

*paintings would give them power
over the animals.*

"Wow, look at this," said Annie.

She pointed at a painting farther down the wall.

It showed a figure with human arms and legs, reindeer antlers, and an owl face. It seemed to be holding a flute.

Jack looked at the book again. He found a picture of the figure and read:

Cave men may have been led by a sorcerer, or "Master of the Animals". He may have worn reindeer antlers so he could run like a reindeer – and an owl mask so he could see like an owl.

"What is it?" said Annie.

"The Master of the Animals," said Jack. "He's a sorcerer."

"Oh wow," breathed Annie. "That's it."

"That's what?"

"That's who we have to find."

"Why?"

"Maybe he's a friend of Morgan's," said Annie.

Jack nodded slowly. "Maybe," he said.

"Let's go and find him," said Annie.

They went back through the tunnel into the first cave.

"We'd better put our lamps back," said Jack.

He and Annie blew out their lamps.

They placed them back by the fire.

Jack's rucksack was on the floor next to the skins. He put the Ice Age book into it.

"How's Peanut?" said Annie.

Jack looked into his pack. "She's not here," he said.

"Oh no!" cried Annie. "She must have crawled out when we were looking at the paintings."

"Peanut!" Jack called.

"Peanut!" called Annie.

Annie walked slowly around the cave, looking into the shadows.

Jack peered around the fire and under each of the furry skins.

"Jack! Come here!" said Annie.

She was standing near the entrance to the cave.

The snow had stopped falling.

In the snow were tiny tracks.

6

Song on the Wind

"Peanut's tracks," said Annie. "We have to find her before she freezes."

She wrapped her reindeer coat around her and headed across the snow.

Jack pulled on his rucksack and followed.

The mouse's tracks led them between the fallen rocks and back on to the open plain.

The wind blew harder. Snow swirled

over the ground, covering the tiny footprints.

"I can't see them any more!" wailed Annie.

She and Jack now stood in the middle of the plain. They stared at the windswept snow.

The mouse's tracks had vanished.

"Yikes," whispered Annie, staring up.

Jack followed her gaze. On one of the cliffs was a tiger. A giant tiger with two long sharp fangs.

"A *sabretooth*," said Jack.

"I hope he doesn't see us," whispered Annie.

"Me too," Jack whispered back. "We'd better head back to the tree house."

Jack and Annie stepped very softly across the snow. Then Jack glanced back at the cliff.

The sabretooth was gone.

"Oh no," he said. "Where is he?"

"Run to the trees!" said Annie.

He and Annie started running. They ran over the snowy plain, heading towards the tall bare trees in the distance.

Suddenly Jack heard a *crack*.

The ground caved in, and Jack went with it.

Annie fell beside him.

They crashed down on to a heap of branches, snow and earth.

They struggled to stand. Jack pushed his glasses into place.

"You all right?" he asked Annie.

"Yes," she said.

They both looked up. They were in a deep hole. All Jack could see were grey clouds moving overhead.

"This is a trap," Jack said. "The Cro-Magnons must have put branches over this hole. Then the snow hid the branches. So we didn't see them."

"There's no way out," said Annie.

She was right. They were helpless. The pit was too deep to climb out of.

"I feel like a trapped animal," Annie said.

"Me too," said Jack.

He heard a yowl in the distance.

"The sabretooth!" whispered Annie.

Jack pulled out the Ice Age book. He found a picture of the sabretooth. He read:

> *The sabretooth was the fiercest beast of the Ice Age. It attacked humans as well as woolly mammoths and other large animals.*

"Oh, just great," said Jack.

"Listen!" Annie grabbed him.

"What?" Jack jumped.

"I hear music."

Jack listened. But all he heard was the wind.

"You hear it?" said Annie.

"No," said Jack.

"Listen carefully."

He closed his eyes. He listened very carefully.

He heard the wind. But this time he heard another sound, too.

Strange, haunting music.

"Ahhh!" cried Annie.

Jack opened his eyes.

Staring down at them was a figure wearing reindeer antlers and an owl mask.

"The sorcerer," whispered Jack.

Squeak.

Peanut peered down at them, too!

7

The Sorcerer's Gift

The sorcerer didn't speak. He stared through the eyeholes of the owl mask.

"Help us, please," said Annie.

The sorcerer threw a rope into the pit. Jack grabbed it.

"He wants to pull us up," said Annie.

Jack looked up. The sorcerer was gone.

"Where did he go?" Jack said.

"Tug on the rope," said Annie.

Jack tugged. The rope tightened. It

began rising.

"I'll go first!" said Annie cheerfully.

"Annie, this isn't a game," warned Jack.

"Don't worry, I'll be careful."

Jack gave her the rope. "Okay. But hold on tight," he said.

Annie held the rope with both hands. She pushed her feet against the side of the pit. She rose into the air with the rope.

She kept pressing against the side of the pit – until she reached the top.

Jack saw the sorcerer reappear and help Annie up. Then they moved out of sight.

Jack was puzzled. The sorcerer had used both hands to help Annie. So who held the other end of the rope?

"Wow!" came Annie's voice.

What's going on? Jack wondered.

The sorcerer came back and threw the rope down again.

Jack grabbed it. And the rope started to rise.

Jack held on tight. He climbed up. His hands burned. His arms felt as if they were being pulled out of their sockets.

But he kept his hold on the rope and his feet against the side of the pit.

At the top the sorcerer pulled Jack on to the snowy ground.

"Thanks," said Jack, standing.

The sorcerer was tall. He wore a long fur robe. Jack could see only his eyes through the owl mask.

"Hey!" Annie called.

Jack turned.

Annie was sitting on a woolly mammoth.

Squeak. Peanut was sitting on the mammoth's head.

The mammoth looked like a giant elephant with shaggy reddish hair and long curved tusks.

The other end of the rope was around

the mammoth's huge neck.

"Lulu pulled us up," said Annie.

"Lulu?" said Jack.

"Don't you think she looks like a Lulu?" said Annie.

"Oh really," said Jack. He walked up to

the mammoth.

"Hey, mammoth starts with M," said
Annie. "Maybe Lulu's the special thing!"

"I don't think so," said Jack.

The great creature knelt down, just
like a circus elephant.

"Whoa!" said Annie. She clutched the mammoth's ears to keep from falling off.

The sorcerer helped Jack climb on to the mammoth.

"Thanks," said Jack.

Then the sorcerer reached into a pouch. He pulled out a smooth white bone and handed it to Jack.

The bone was hollow. It had four holes along one side. And two on the other.

"Oh cool, I think it's his flute," said Jack. "The book said they make flutes from mammoth bones."

Jack tried to give the flute back to the sorcerer.

"Nice," he said politely.

But the sorcerer held up his hand.

"He wants you to keep the mammoth bone," said Annie.

"*Mammoth bone*," whispered Jack. "Hey, maybe this is the third thing."

Jack looked at the sorcerer. "Do you

know Morgan?" he asked.

The sorcerer did not answer. But his eyes sparkled with kindness.

He turned away from Jack and untied the mammoth's rope. Then he whispered in the ear of the giant woolly creature.

When the mammoth stood up, Jack gripped Annie's coat to keep from falling off. He felt miles above the ground.

He nestled behind Annie, in the dip between the mammoth's head and huge curved back.

The mammoth took slow plodding steps across the snow, then picked up speed.

"Where are we going?" said Jack as they bumped up and down.

"To the tree house!" said Annie.

"How does he know where it is?" said Jack.

"*She* just knows," said Annie.

Jack looked back.

The sorcerer was standing in the snow, watching them.

But at that moment the clouds parted, and the sun came out.

Jack was blinded by sunlight on the snow.

He squinted to see – but the sorcerer had vanished.

8

The Great Parade

The huge mammoth walked across the open plain.

"Look!" said Annie. She pointed to a herd of elk in the distance. They had great wide antlers.

"There!" said Jack as a herd of reindeer came into view. They pranced gracefully across the snow.

Then a woolly rhino joined them on the open plain. Then a bison!

The elk, reindeer, rhino and bison moved along with them, at a distance.

They seemed to be escorting Jack and Annie back to the tree house.

The snow sparkled with sunlight.

This is a great parade, Jack thought. *Fantastic.*

They were getting closer and closer to the grove of tall trees.

"I told you," said Annie. "Lulu's taking us home."

But just then the mammoth let out a cry. All the other animals bounded off.

Peanut started to squeak.

Jack looked around.

Behind them the sabretooth was slinking across the sunlit snow!

The woolly mammoth roared and plunged forward.

Jack and Annie nearly fell off.

Jack clutched Annie. She and Peanut clutched the mammoth's shaggy hair.

The mammoth thundered wildly over the ground.

"Ahhh!" Jack and Annie yelled.

The mammoth charged to the grove of trees.

But the tiger had circled around the trees. He stood between the tallest tree

and the mammoth.

They were trapped.

The sabretooth began moving slowly towards the mammoth.

The woolly mammoth roared fiercely.

But Jack knew a sabretooth could kill any creature, including a mammoth.

The huge tiger's head was down. His burning eyes were fixed on the mammoth. His long white fangs glinted in the sunlight.

9

Master of the Animals

The sabretooth crept forwards.

Jack stared in horror.

"Play the flute," whispered Annie.

Is she nuts? Jack thought.

"Try!" said Annie.

Jack held the mammoth-bone flute to his lips. He blew.

The flute made a strange sound.

The tiger froze. He glared at Jack.

Jack's hands shook.

The tiger growled. He took another step.

The mammoth roared and stomped the ground.

"Play it!" said Annie. "Keep playing!"

Jack blew again.

The sabretooth froze again.

Jack kept blowing until he ran out of breath.

The tiger snarled.

"He's still here," whispered Annie. "Keep it up."

Jack closed his eyes. He took a deep breath. Then he blew as hard and as long as he could. He covered and uncovered the holes on the bone.

The music sounded strange – as if it were coming from another world.

"He's leaving!" Annie whispered.

Jack raised his eyes. The sabretooth was slinking off towards the cliffs.

"We did it!" said Annie.

Jack lowered the flute. He felt very tired.

The mammoth waved her trunk happily.

"To the tree house, Lulu," said Annie.

The woolly mammoth snorted. Then she lumbered over to the tallest tree.

From the back of the mammoth, Jack grabbed the rope-ladder. He held it for Annie.

She stroked the mammoth's giant ear. "Bye, Lulu. Thank you," she said.

Annie grabbed the rope ladder. Then she climbed up. Peanut climbed up, too.

After they disappeared into the tree house, Jack climbed on to the ladder.

He looked back at the woolly mammoth. "Bye, girl," he said. "Go home now. And watch out for the sabretooth."

The mammoth walked away into the sunset.

When Jack couldn't see her any more,

he climbed up the rope-ladder. He pulled himself into the tree house.

"Ta-da!" said Annie. She handed the Pennsylvania book to Jack.

Jack smiled. Now he was positive they had found the third M thing. Their mission was complete.

"Before we leave, we have to give our coats back," said Annie.

"Oh, right," said Jack.

They took off their reindeer-skin coats and dropped them to the ground.

"Brrr!" said Annie. "I hope the Cro-Magnon people find them."

Jack stared out of the window. He wanted to take one last look at the prehistoric world.

The sun was setting behind the hills. Four people were crossing the snowy plain. It was the Cro-Magnon family.

"Hey!" shouted Annie.

"Shhh!" said Jack.

The Cro-Magnons stopped and peered in Annie and Jack's direction.

"We left your reindeer skins! Down there!" Annie pointed to the ground.

The tallest person stepped forward and raised a spear.

"Time to go," said Jack.

He grabbed the Pennsylvania book. He found the picture of Frog Creek and pointed at it. "I wish we could go home," he said.

"Goodbye! Good luck!" Annie called, waving out of the window.

The wind started to blow.

The leaves began to shake.

The wind blew harder. And the tree house started to spin.

It spun faster and faster.

Then everything was still.

Absolutely still.

10

This Age

Birds sang. The air was soft and warm.

"I hope they find their coats," said Annie.

"Me too," said Jack. He pushed his glasses into place.

Squeak.

"Hey, you – how did you find the sorcerer?" Annie asked Peanut.

Squeak.

"It's a secret, huh?" said Annie. She

turned to Jack. "Where's the flute?"

He held up the mammoth bone. Then he placed it on the M carved into the floor. Next to the mango from the rain forest. Next to the moonstone from the time of ninjas.

"Moonstone, mango, mammoth bone . . ." Annie said. "We need just one more M thing. Then Morgan will be free from her spell."

"Tomorrow," said Jack.

Annie patted Peanut on the head. "Bye, you," she said.

She climbed down the rope-ladder.

Jack gathered his things.

He paused and glanced at the mouse. She stared at him with big brown eyes.

"Thanks again for helping us," he said.

Then he climbed down the rope ladder and jumped on to the ground.

Jack and Annie ran through the Frog Creek woods on to their street.

Their neighbourhood looked rosy in the sunset.

It's great to be back in this age, Jack thought. *Warm and safe and almost home.*

"I'm glad we don't have to go hunting for dinner," he said.

"Yeah, Mum and Dad already did that," said Annie, "at the supermarket."

"I hope they trapped some spaghetti and meatballs," said Jack.

"I hope they trapped a pizza," said Annie.

"Hurry, I'm starving," said Jack.

They ran up their pavement and through their front door.

"We're home!" shouted Annie.

"What's for dinner?" shouted Jack.

"Race you!" said Annie.

They took off running.

They ran across their garden.

They raced up their steps.

"Safe!" they shouted together, tagging their front door.

MAGIC TREE HOUSE

If you love reading all about Jack and Annie's adventures then you'll want to join the

MAGIC TREE HOUSE CLUB

Members will receive:

* A reading ladder to keep a record of the books you have read. Make sure you save the token below for this.

* A membership card and newsletters.

* Exclusive news and freebies!

To join the club send your full name and address, with the signature of your parent / guardian to:

**The Magic Tree House Club
Publicity Dept, Scholastic Children's Books,
Commonwealth House, 1-19 New Oxford Street,
London WC1A 1NU.**

(membership packs cannot be sent out without a parental signature)

Adventure is waiting inside every Magic Tree House Book!

**READING
LADDER
TOKEN**

YOUng HiPPO

More brilliant story books to collect from Young Hippo:

Royal Blunder
Royal Blunder &
the Haunted House
Henrietta Branford

School Poems
Jennifer Curry

Christmas Quackers
Sylvia Green

Broomstick Services
Broomstick Removals
Broomstick Rescues
Broomstick Baby
Ann Jungman

Bobby the Bad
Warlock Watson
What Sadie Saw
Dick King-Smith

Bursting Balloons Mystery
Chocolate Money Mystery
The Bubblegum Tree
The Popcorn Pirates
Alexander McCall Smith

The Ghost in the Telly
Frank Rodgers

Young Hippo Big Books

The Big Book of Dragons
The Big Haunted House Book
The Big Magic Animal Book
The Big Wicked Witch Book
The Big Bad School Book
The Big Animal Ghost Book